THE KING WHO WANTED TO SEE GOD

By Richard Matsuura, Ph.D.
Ruth Matsuura, M.D.

Illustrated by Linus Chao

ORCHID ISLE PUBLISHING CO.
131 HALAI STREET
HILO, HAWAII 96720

TO THE CHILDREN OF HAWAII
AND MISS RUTH ITAMURA

Library of Congress Catalog
Card Number 95-70923

THE KING WHO WANTED TO SEE GOD

Once there lived a wealthy King in a far away country. He was a very religious man and had a great desire to see and hear the voice of God.

The King built magnificent churches and temples. He brought wise men from the far corners of the world to share with him any personal knowledge or experience of God.

One of the wise men mentioned about a boy, blind from birth, who could speak five different languages. This impressed the King and had the blind boy brought to him. In talking to the blind boy, the King found that the boy had merely memorized poems and speeches in five different languages. "Anyone could do that," remarked the King and continued his search for God.

Another wise man told the King of a Holy man who lived and meditated in the snowcapped areas in the Himalayan mountains. "People say that he could walk on water," said the wise man.

"Arrange to have that man brought to me at once", requested the King. "I will reward him handsomely."

The wise man stroked his white beard and murmured, "He will not come. He has no use for earthly things. If you wish to see him, you must go to him. I will arrange a guide to take you deep into the Himalayan mountain."

The King was reluctant to go but agreed to take the journey. After months of traveling, the King finally found the Holy man sitting in front of a waterfall.

The Holy man had his eyes closed in meditation. The King introduced himself, but the Holy man remained in silent meditation. The King angrily demanded that he talk to him. The Holy man opened his eyes and looked at the King very carefully. The King in a loud voice repeated that he is the King. The Holy man replied, "So you are the King."

The King asked, "Have you seen or heard God?"

A smile crossed the Holy man's face and he replied, "No. Have you?" the King walked away very disappointed.

The King pursued his search to the four corners of the world. He sat many days under the Bodhi tree where Gautama Buddha was enlightened. He visited the Holy lands in Jerusalem, retracing the path Jesus of Nazareth took. He meditated in a mosque in Mecca. However, he had never seen or heard of God.

His search continued for many years; and in his ailing old age, he had given up all hope of attaining his one and only goal, to see or hear God. The King became ill. As he lay on his death bed, he heard the voices of children coming through the window. Their laughter and singing brought tears to his eyes. The King asked to have the children brought to his bedroom.

All the children bowed in respect and approached the King cautiously. The King said, "All my life I sought to see or hear God, but I have never seen God."

"I have," replied a young girl.

The King motioned her to come closer. "You have seen God?" he asked.

"Yes," she said. "God is everywhere."

"Could you show me so I, too, may see Him?" requested the King.

The little girl opened the window and pointed, "There is God. He is everywhere!"

The King was helped to the window. "Where?" he asked.

The little girl replied, "Look at the trees, the birds, the mountain, the flowers. That is God's work."

The King went back to his bed disappointed. "I thought that you had actually seen God in person." The King then asked the littlest boy to sit next to him. "Have you seen God?" asked the King.

"Nope," was the boy's immediate reply.

The King asked, "Would you want to see Him?"

"Nope," the boy replied.

"Why not?" asked the King.

The little boy hesitated for a moment and replied, "Because I don't know Him."

The King laughed until tears were running down his cheeks. He turned to his counselors and said, "All my life I searched for God. I traveled the four corners of the world looking for God. And now in my dying days, in my bedroom, I see God all around me."

The King commanded, "Call all my counselors, the Queen and my children for I want to share that which I devoted a lifetime."

When everyone was gathered around the King, he claimed, "There will come a time when God will appear in a form that we can see Him; but if I were to reconstruct that God as a person, He would have these characteristics. He would be humble and trusting like a child, loving as a mother of a newborn child, and forgiving as a grandparent. In essence, like the little girl said, 'God is everywhere. We must just recognize the good in everything and in every person.'"

When the King died, on the tombstone was written, "A man who looked for God and found Him in every good person."

THE END

ABOUT THE AUTHORS

Richard M. Matsuura, Ph.D.
> Born in Waialua, Oahu, Hawaii
> Graduated from Waialua High School
> Attended Oregon State University, B.S.
> University of Minnesota, Ph.D. in Horticulture
> Attended Bethel Theological Seminary, St. Paul, Minnesota

Ruth M. Matsuura, M.D.
> Born in Hanford, California
> Graduated from Hanford High School
> Attended University of California, Berkeley, B.A.
> University of California School of Medicine, San Francisco, M.D.

Missionaries under United Presbyterian Church, USA to India, 1961-1971

Richard served in the Hawaii State Legislature in the House of Representatives, 1980 to 1984, and the State Senate from 1984 to present.

Ruth is in private pediatric practice from 1971 to present.

Married; six children.

ABOUT THE ILLUSTRATOR
LINUS CHAO

Linus is a native of Shantung, North China. In 1955, he graduated from the Fine Arts Department of the National Normal University in Taipei, Taiwan. He studied visual arts in Tokyo, animation art at the University of Southern California and at Walt Disney Studio. He earned a Master of Science degree in art education from Bank Street College and Parsons School of Design in New York City.

Linus has won several international awards and has published many art books. His work has been displayed at several International Art Festivals in Taiwan, China, Brazil, Montreal, San Francisco and Hawaii.

Linus teaches art at the Hawaii Community College. His wife, Jane, is also an outstanding artist. Their paintings hang in museums and private collections in North and South America, Europe and Asia.

Other books published by Richard and Ruth Matsuura,
illustrated by Linus Chao:

Hawaiian Christmas Story
The Fruit, The Tree, The Flower
Kalani and Primo
The Birthday Wish
Alii Kai
A Gift from Santa
Angels Masquerading on Earth